Favorite Thing of All

Written by Keith Ogorek
Illustrated by Heather Ray Boelke

AuthorHouse™
1663 Liberty Drive
Bloomington, IN 47403
www.authorhouse.com
Phone: 833-262-8899

Because of the dynamic nature of the Internet, any web addresses or links contained in this book may have changed
since publication and may no longer be valid. The views expressed in this work are solely those of the author and do
not necessarily reflect the views of the publisher, and the publisher hereby disclaims any responsibility for them.

Any people depicted in stock imagery provided by Getty Images are models,
and such images are being used for illustrative purposes only.
Certain stock imagery © Getty Images.

This book is printed on acid-free paper.

ISBN: 979-8-8230-1727-5 (sc)
ISBN: 979-8-8230-1728-2 (e)

Library of Congress Control Number: 2023921421

Print information available on the last page.

Published by AuthorHouse 11/03/2023

authorHOUSE®

We can go to the zoo

Or play peek-a-boo

We can go to the park

Or count stars when it's dark

We can take a long walk
Or just sit and talk

We can play in the sand
Or pretend we're in a band

But no matter where we are
No matter what we do
My favorite thing of all

Is spending time with you

We can fly
in a plane

Or play out in the rain

We can stack up blocks
Or put your toys in a box

We can draw a square
Or growl like a bear

We can swim in a lake

Or even bake a cake

But no matter where we are
No matter what we do
My favorite thing of all
Is spending time with you

So many places to go
So many things to do
But none of them are as special
As spending time with you

So no matter where we are
No matter what we do
My favorite thing of all
Is spending time with you

Printed in the United States
by Baker & Taylor Publisher Services